Oak Park Public Library

3 1132 01350 6211

MAY

W9-BEY-508

OAK PARK PUBLIC LIBRARY

汝作虹橋夢吾亦迎頭喜
汝若為暴雨吾以山谷接
汝若霹靂雷吾以手掩耳
汝若現雲霞吾化成萬泉
汝若為煙霧吾助上昇天
汝若一堆火吾以火爐盛
汝卧冷沙灘吾供火取暖
汝若起微波吾為淺岸接
汝若為輕風吾作漣漪洄
汝若大森林吾以風動搖
汝若一題子吾仰望高枝
汝為明湖鏡吾即鏡中影
汝若挂高瀑吾當喊求救
汝若為川澗吾寧實急流

Be a River

a poem about

ED YOUNG

LITTLE, BROWN AND COMPANY

New York   Boston

Should you be a river,

I'll race your rapids downstream.

Should you be a waterfall.

I'll scream when you plunge.

Should you be a calm lake,
I'll hold you,

reflecting your
every move.

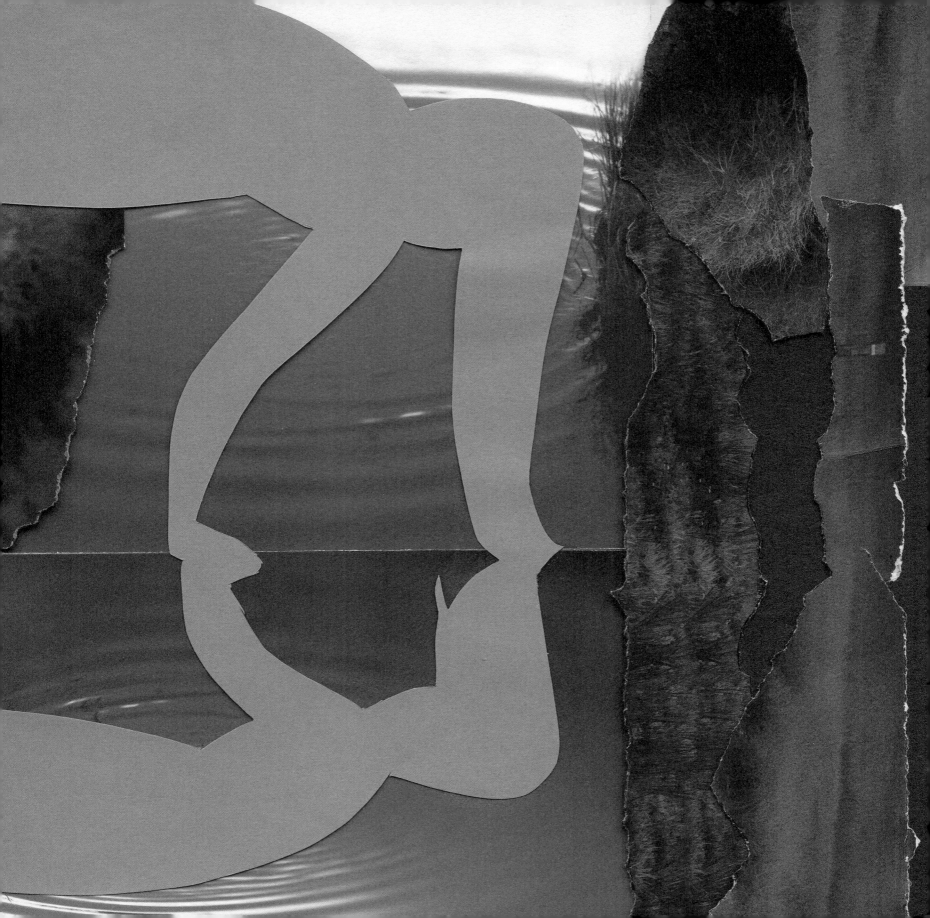

Should you be a seed,

I'll dream you a vision of towering trees,

Should you be a great forest,

I'll caress your branches and make you sway.

Should you be a breeze, I'll be ripples

Should you be a gentle wave,
I'll wait for you to lap my shores,

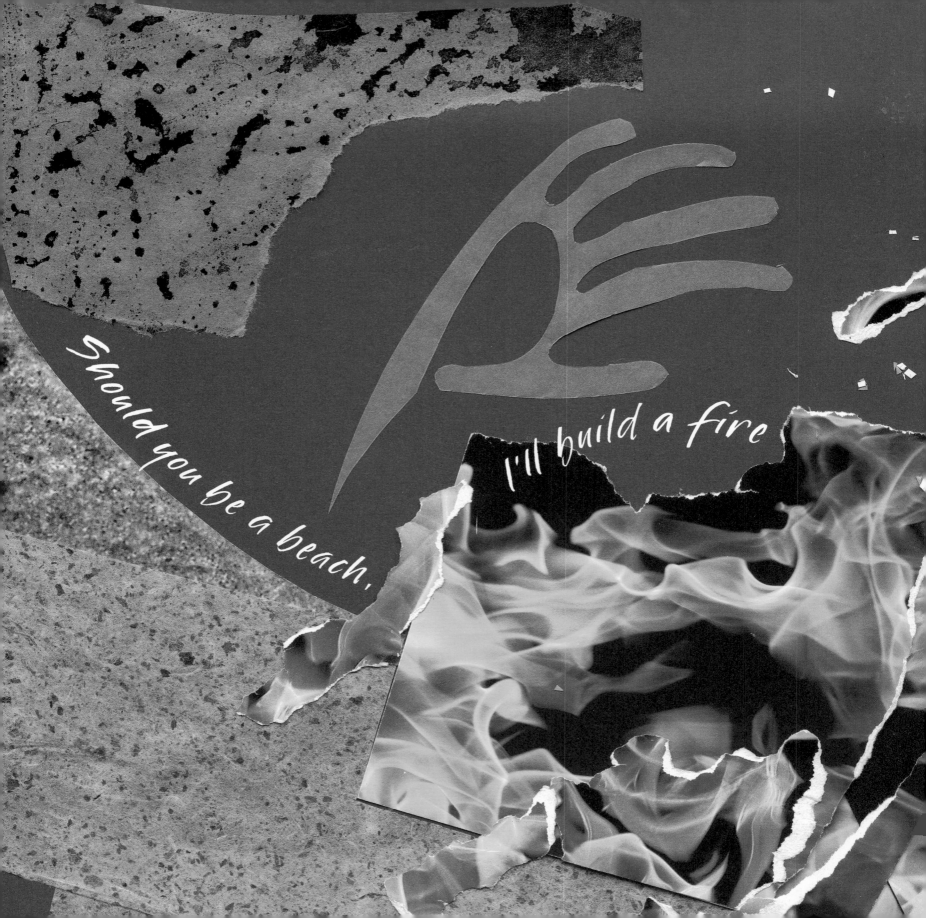

Should you be a beach,

I'll build a fire

to keep you warm.

should you be a vaporous smoke.

Should you be a cloud,

I'll imagine you in countless fantastical forms.

Should you be a rain shower,

I'll be a gentle valley to receive you.

Should you be a rainbow,

Should you be a river...

AUTHOR'S NOTE

In 2007, my two daughters were at the ages of eleven and thirteen when their mother passed away. I was painfully aware of my limited capabilities as a substitute provider. However, we did what we had to as a threesome in regard to household chores—cooking, cleaning, laundry—and carpools to and from school, thirty miles away from home.

Two years ago, in a casual conversation, my younger daughter revealed a sentiment of recently having gotten over missing her mom. That revelation triggered an awareness of my role as a single parent.

On the very next morning, the lines of this book were floating in my waking mind. I jotted them down in my journal and shared them with a few friends. My photographer friend Sean Kernan expressed an interest in using his nature photography as collage in collaboration with the words. The idea grew into a scroll forty feet long. We were envisioning it as a piece for a gallery wall, with Chinese translation written in Sean's hand alongside the art.

As one never knows what one's future holds, the poem became mixed up in an envelope I used to send my art for *Nighttime Ninja* to Little, Brown. My art director, Patti Ann Harris, discovered it and shared it with my editor, Alvina Ling. They made an offer to publish it as a picture book for all ages.

In the book's final stage, I invited my calligrapher friend Barbara Bash to come on board to round out my vision for a true collaboration on a labor of love. There are no words to express my feeling of gratitude for everyone who has come into my life to make this book possible.

—Ed Young

That WISDOM
which gives
each egg
its color, texture, and pattern of
the vulnerable, open habitat
where it is laid,
so it might survive harm.

—Ed Young

About This Book

This book was edited by Alvina Ling and designed by Patti Ann Harris. The production was supervised by Erika Schwartz, and the production editor was Barbara Bakowski. This book was printed on 140-gsm Gold Sun wood-free paper. The text is hand-lettered calligraphy by Barbara Bash. The illustrations for this book were done in cut-paper collage, including nature photography by Sean Kernan.

Copyright © 2015 by Ed Young • Cover art © 2015 by Ed Young • Cover design by Patti Ann Harris • Cover © 2015 Hachette Book Group, Inc. • All rights reserved. In accordance with the U.S. Copyright Act of 1976, the scanning, uploading, and electronic sharing of any part of this book without the permission of the publisher is unlawful piracy and theft of the author's intellectual property. If you would like to use material from the book (other than for review purposes), prior written permission must be obtained by contacting the publisher at permissions@hbgusa.com. Thank you for your support of the author's rights.
 • Little, Brown and Company • Hachette Book Group • 1290 Avenue of the Americas, New York, NY 10104 • Visit our website at lb-kids.com • Little, Brown and Company is a division of Hachette Book Group, Inc. • The Little, Brown name and logo are trademarks of Hachette Book Group, Inc. • The publisher is not responsible for websites (or their content) that are not owned by the publisher. • First Edition: April 2015 • Library of Congress Cataloging-in-Publication Data • Young, Ed. Should you be a river : a poem about love/ by Ed Young. — 1st ed. • pages cm • Summary: "A personally inspired poem that celebrates the trials and triumphs of unconditional love"— Provided by publisher. • ISBN 978-0-316-23089-6 (hardcover) • [1. Love—Fiction.] I. Title. • PZ7.Y85Sh 2015 • [E]—dc23 • 2013043172 • 10 9 8 7 6 5 4 3 2 1 • SC • Printed in China

SHOULD YOU BE A RIVER, I'LL RACE YOUR RAPIDS DOWNSTREAM.

SHOULD YOU BE A WATERFALL, I'LL SCREAM WHEN YOU PLUNGE.

SHOULD YOU BE A CALM LAKE, I'LL HOLD YOU, REFLECTING YOUR EVERY MOVE.

SHOULD YOU BE A SEED, I'LL DREAM YOU A VISION OF TOWERING TREES.

SHOULD YOU BE A GREAT FOREST, I'LL CARESS YOUR BRANCHES AND MAKE YOU SWAY.

SHOULD YOU BE A BREEZE, I'LL BE RIPPLES DANCING TO YOUR TUNES.

SHOULD YOU BE A GENTLE WAVE, I'LL WAIT FOR YOU TO LAP MY SHORES.

SHOULD YOU BE A BEACH, I'LL BUILD A FIRE TO KEEP YOU WARM.

SHOULD YOU BE A FLAME, I'LL HOLD YOU SNUGLY IN MY HEARTH.

SHOULD YOU BE A VAPOROUS SMOKE, I'LL LIFT YOU TO TOUCH THE HEAVENS.

SHOULD YOU BE A CLOUD, I'LL IMAGINE YOU IN COUNTLESS FANTASTICAL FORMS.

SHOULD YOU BE THUNDER, I'LL HOLD MY BREATH, HANDS OVER MY EARS.

SHOULD YOU BE A RAIN SHOWER, I'LL BE A GENTLE VALLEY TO RECEIVE YOU.

SHOULD YOU BE A RAINBOW, I'LL BE AN ARROW SOARING TO JOIN YOUR LUMINOUS HUES.

SHOULD YOU BE A RIVER...